"A master of mood, seamlessly combining the literary with the grotesque. Johnson deserves to be a household name…"
—*Publishers Weekly*

"Genre-bending…haunting…"
—*The Washington Post*

"Johnson captures humanity's absurdity, our grotesqueries, sometimes our triumphs, all the while pushing past the limits of reality, transforming it into something dark, and surreal, and unforgettable."
—*B&N Sci-Fi & Fantasy Blog*

"A powerful imagination, a great talent for storytelling, writing chops that allow him to tackle any genre, and a flowing, dynamic voice that, if Johnson were a singer, would extend to an impressive eight octaves."
—*Electric Literature*

"Surreal, visceral, and frequently unsettling…One more descriptor, while we're at it: highly entertaining. Johnson brings a pulpy urgency to the page, which blends neatly with the frequently heady concepts that he utilizes in his fiction."
—*Tor.com*

"Johnson writes with an energy that propels you through some very dark spaces indeed and into some-

thing profoundly unsettling but nonetheless human."
—**Brian Evenson, author of** *A Collapse of Horses*

"Reading Johnson, you feel you are in the grip of an immensely powerful, possibly malevolent, but fiercely intelligent mind."
—**Nick Cutter, author of** *The Troop*

"I've seen the future and it's bizarre, it's beautifully berserk, it's Jeremy Robert Johnson."
—**Stephen Graham Jones, author of** *Mongrels*

"A dazzling writer."
—**Chuck Palahniuk, author of** *Fight Club*

"One of the most exciting voices in contemporary fiction. Jeremy Robert Johnson's work has always tested the limits of both genre and literary fiction."
—*Bookslut*

"Not unlike David Foster Wallace's wicked and perhaps deranged younger brother."
—*21C Magazine*

"The guy's a genius. Reminds me of William Gibson—the dark interest in altered states of consciousness, the unrelentingly furious forward movement, and the same kind of unlimited imagination."
—**Ben Loory, author of** *Stories for Nighttime and Some for the Day*

"Johnson weaves vivid and fascinatingly grotesque tales."
—*Bookgasm*

In the River

Jeremy Robert Johnson

Lazy Fascist Press
an imprint of Eraserhead Press

ISBN: 978-1-62105-251-7

For Donna J. Johnson,
who made me and saved me,
and sent me the message reading:

SOMETIMES THINGS ARE BEYOND
OUR CONTROL.

The man and boy approached the river and saw it as it had been for generations: a place which offered them life. But the boy must have noticed the violent swirl in the deep of mid-river and the way the once-clear shallows had been churned dark by the morning's rain. He halted along the trail.

"Dad?"

The man turned and saw his son—skin darker and hair lighter from a summer's sun spent at play, body stretched thin and tall, the last of his baby fat burned, the early angles of a man's face emerging though the boy had only seven years—and he felt something pull in his heart, an urge to embrace the boy and lift him from his feet and quiet his worry. But the man had learned to fish at seven, and so would the boy, and the time for coddling had passed.

"Yes?"

"River looks rough."

"It will calm by mid-day. We'll have good fishing. Now tighten the straps on your pack or it will jostle on the hike down and rub you raw."

The boy pulled the straps tighter and stood taller, reminded of the privilege of carrying a portion of their gear for the first time. His worrying passed and he ran down the steep dirt trail to the side of the river.

The boy reached bottom first and pulled deep breaths of the cool clean river air. He un-bunched his tan shorts—all that either he or the man would bother to wear this time of year, especially knowing they'd be in and out of the river—and kicked off his shoes and stepped toward the stony shallows.

"Stop!"

The boy edged closer, always pushing.

"I said, "Stop!"" The man was louder, searching for the tone which would actually halt the boy. The boy threw his hands in the air, frustrated at having his urge denied. But he had stopped.

The man finally reached the edge of the river and he was quickly to his son and he put his hands on the boy's shoulders.

"If you're going to learn this, you have to listen. You will listen."

"I'm listening. I promise. Will I get to use the bow?"

"Not today."

"Mom said I'd get to use the bow."

The man pictured the arrow in his younger brother's side, how his parents had ceased noticing he existed until the wooden tip was removed and the village doctor demanded that all three of them hold shut the wound. He remembered how his brother had cried out as the doctor applied each soldier ant, allowing their massive mandibles to latch and bind the torn flesh, and how the doctor twisted away at each ant's torso until only the head remained to hold the lockjaw suture. He'd told his parents it was an accident—that he'd slipped on the rocks with his bow already drawn—but it took so long for their eyes to soften to him again.

"No. No bow today. Let's see how you fare with the nets first, huh?"

"I want to cool down in the river."

"What do we always do first?"

The boy kicked at the ground and growled. Small

stones skittered and splashed into the water.

"What do we always do?"

The boy let go of a final huff and met the man's eyes. "We clear the banks."

The man gave the boy's shoulders a squeeze. "Yes. We clear the banks. Now pass me your gear and find us two long sticks along the base of the hill."

The boy set to work searching and the man sorted their supplies in a clearing, spreading out nets and vine-bound bamboo arrows and salty smoked fish and two bags of boiled water and a small container of milk he'd bought from the peddler as a surprise for the boy.

He told the boy exactly what to pack—essentials only—so he was confused by the object at the bottom of the boy's bag until he brought it to light. Micho, the great black cat, a teething doll the boy's mother had made for him. It smelled of the boy, the way his warm breath or the back of his head smelled when he jumped into the man's lap in the morning.

Micho was not essential, but the man let it pass. He turned his head toward the breaking clouds and felt warmth on his face.

The boy yelled, "I'm going to find the two best sticks!" and the man knew that this was going to be a fine day.

"Keep it as far out in front of you as you can and sweep it back and forth like this."

"Like this?"

"No. A little bit deeper. Sometimes they float just past the break and poke their snouts up for breath."

The black caiman crocs weren't as heavy along the banks this time of year—breeding season had carried them further upriver—but they were still a danger. And once the paraja leaves were submerged and the fish had slowed, the crocs would have an easy time stripping the harvest.

"If I hit one with my stick, won't he be angry?"

"Sure he will. That's why it's a long stick."

The man thought the boy might laugh, but he looked back to see a serious, furrowed brow.

"You hit him with that stick, first thing he'll do

is let you know he's there. Might thrash his head or hiss or even snap. But you'll know he's there, and he'll know you know it, and that makes him think twice. He's a sneaky old lizard. A coward. He wants to catch his prey unsuspecting so they can't fight."

The man thought of his cousin, stark white, leg gone below the hip, laid to rest in the family grove beyond their village.

He looked to the boy and saw his eyes were wide and pinned to every movement of the river. The man decided that the boy understood. He'd save his cousin's story and the fear it carried for another time when the boy looked more reckless.

"And what else are we checking for?"

"Eel brood. Piranha. Um…"

"There's one we listen for. It's a big one."

"Oh…um…it's ara…ara…I can't get it."

"You almost got it. Arapaima. Fish too big to breathe underwater. You can hear him when he pushes his head above the river to gulp at the air. He's got a tongue with its own set of teeth, remember? But if we hear one we head back to the village as fast as we can, and see if we can hunt him as a team. Arapaima means we eat for a week, so long as he doesn't get us first."

The man looked back and the boy was still all seriousness. Perhaps that was better, that he was like his mother in that way. The river gave so much to them, but the river was also serious.

"You're doing a good job, kid."

The boy beamed and swept the water with greater intent.

The boy was impatient and grew tired of clearing the shore after an hour. The man, too, was impatient. The sun was beginning to crest and the paraja leaves would be most effective in the heat. They'd found no crocs, even after locating a shallow crossing upstream and checking the opposite bank.

"We can fish now?"

"Yes. Help me set the leaves."

The paraja leaves had been dried and bagged last week and sat in a small bamboo hutch the man's village kept by the river. Only a few bags would be needed to slow the fish. Today's harvest would be small, a lesson more than anything.

The sun beat on their brown backs as they hiked upriver and built submerged rock cairns around seven of the bags. They stopped to splash each other with cool water and drank deeply from the bag they'd brought.

"Can't we just drink from the river? It's right here."

"Always better boiled. Too many villages above ours. And right now, with those paraja leaves in the stream, your legs would go numb in an hour and you'd end up laid out sick."

"Dead sick?"

Always, a small shock went through the man when the boy mentioned death aloud.

"No, only wishing it. Your legs burn like fire when the feeling comes back."

"Oh." The boy stood straighter and veered toward a shallow part of the bank.

"It's okay, kid. It won't get in through your skin."

Something jumped from branch to branch in the

tree above them and tiny seeds swirled down to the river, hundreds of them backlit by a hot white sun.

Back at the clearing the man showed the boy how to use rocks to pin nets across the river. How to create ever-more shallow stone inlets which would drive the slowed fish into those nets. How to create a stone pool to keep their live catch fresh until sunset.

The boy worked valiantly—the man knew that he would sleep late tomorrow and feel the wonderful ache of true work for the first time.

And when their first fish—a yellow-gold tucunare the size of the man's hand—drifted through their stone trap and wriggled in their net, the boy yelled, "We got it! We got it!" and the man lifted him and spun him in circles until he felt the boy might take wing.

The man returned the boy to earth. "Do you think that little fish is enough for dinner?"

"No!"

"So let's catch some more."

Within two hours they had eight fish in their pond, including a huge jacunda that the man had to further stun with a rock to keep it from eating the rest of their catch. The day's work had them spent and so they sat in the early afternoon shade and shared chunks of salted fish and a handful of nuts and drained the remaining boiled water. Then the man surprised the boy with the milk he'd bought from the peddler.

"It's good?"

The boy hesitated. "Yes."

Normally the boy would have been joyous. Milk was rare and his favorite. But it was rumored that the peddler had hit hard times and was hiding water on his person to mix with the milk right before he gave it to you. Perhaps it was true.

If so, that meant that the boy cared for his father's feelings, but it also meant that he was learning to lie. At this rate he'd be a man too soon.

The man wondered later, a thousand times, maybe more, "What would have happened if I'd brought more water for our trip?" But he hadn't, and he was proud, and tired, and busy cleaning the day's catch, and he couldn't have known how hot the day's sun would be, or how hard-working and thirsty and forgetful his son would be while retrieving their nets, or how quiet the boy might have been when he bent to the leaf-poisoned river and cupped his hands and brought the water to his mouth and drank it down.

He couldn't have known all this, and he didn't, so when the boy returned to the clearing and picked up the man's bow and arrow and said, "Please" the man said, "Yes. Only once. Then we're headed home."

At the time, the smile on that boy's face was the sun.

"This will be harder now that the light is fading. You can see them best when the sun shines straight down past the tree break. As the light bends, so will the way you see the fish."

"What?"

"It's…hard to explain. You'll learn it by feel. By practice. I may have taken a hundred shots before I managed to hit my first one."

They stepped further toward mid-river. The man wondered if this was too soon, but the boy planted each foot slow and sturdy and he kept the bow pointed down and away.

"What am I looking for, dad?"

"Movement. Color. Something that will betray the fish. And when you see him, you hold still and stiff as a tree and lift a free hand to tell me to do the same."

The boy was intent, scanning left to right, moving further from the bank. At knee depth the man felt the warmth of the shallows recede. The river bottom grew softer. Plumes of silt and sand and dead brown leaves rose around each foot. Even this late in the season there was a cold current beneath the surface.

The boy watched the river. The man watched the boy—further out, moving with a slowness that was almost odd, thinking only of the hunt. The water was to the man's hips now, and the boy's chest, gooseflesh tightening across them both. Each step had to be recalibrated. Moving forward meant leaning your weight against the current.

The boy's left hand rose. He'd spotted something.

The boy's left hand was shaking.

"It's a big one, dad! It just swam past. So big. Could be a…ara…"

"Arapaima?"

The man doubted they'd have such luck, but he slowly stepped toward his son.

"So big, dad. I swear. But I can't see it now."

An early evening wind blew across the river, swaying the trees, their dry leaves rattling against each other. The boy shivered. Even after the shiver subsided, there was still a tremor to the child's body. He shook in a way the man hadn't seen before. The river was much colder here. There was a splash to their left, something breaking the surface for a moment then diving back down.

There was no gulping sound as the great fish surfaced. What the boy had seen was not an arapaima.

They needed to return to the riverbank.

The man scanned the surface of the water and moved to the boy as quickly as he could.

"Hand me the bow, now!"

"I…"

"We need to get to the bank, as fast as we can. Hand me the goddamn bow!"

Could he even defend them with the bow? What had the boy seen? The wind was whipping over the surface of the river and the bottom had begun to roil. The man looked around them again, then back to the boy who looked to be on the edge of tears.

"I can't, dad."

"Can't what? This is no time to…"

"I couldn't hold the bow anymore. I…"

The man looked past the boy and saw the bow and arrow bobbing along the blackwater south of them, then back to the boy and saw he was breathing in short, fast gulps, his chest nearly submerged. The boy's arms had dropped into the river and swayed to his side with the current.

"My hands, dad, they barely…I can't."

"It doesn't matter. Damn it. Get to the bank. Be quick. Stay on my left."

"Dad…it's in my legs too…" There was a panic

descending into the boy's voice.

"What?"

"MY LEGS, DAD!"

And the boy began to cry because he knew what he'd done, and he knew it was bad once he remembered what his father had said about drinking from the river, but now it was too late and he was scared and he needed help. The father saw all of this on his face in less than a moment, and somewhere at the back of his mind he could feel that something was watching them, so all was forgiven and the only thing that mattered was getting back to land.

The man's first instinct was to get the boy out of the water. He remembered how easily he'd carried the boy on long hikes beyond their village, how the boy sat on his shoulders like a king. The pride he'd felt.

He looked the boy in the eyes—the child needed to understand what was happening, to not be afraid and help however he could.

"I'll carry you."

The man took in a deep breath and dove into the river and swam behind his son, then used his arms to propel his body down to where he could push himself between his son's thighs and get his feet beneath him. He pushed up and the muddy river floor opened beneath their combined weight and sucked at the man's legs, but his head broke the surface and all but his son's feet were out of the water and there was an immediate relief in that.

It's a big one, Dad! It just swam past. So big.

Get out of the river.

The boy's weight pushed down on the man, shifting forward, slumping against the back of his head with a deadweight ballast the man normally only felt when the boy fell asleep in his arms.

"I can't feel my body, dad. I can't feel it." The boy's voice closer to hysteria.

Please don't scream. Something is listening.

The man's hands were iron-shackle tight around the boy's ankles. He was certain there'd be bruises later.

"It's okay. I've got you, buddy. I've got you."

Another step forward, and another, and time could not have moved slower in the man's mind, each second and each step stretched too long and the riverbank looking forever distant, and then the boy screamed as if branded and the man looked to his right in time to see the tail of some great fish sweeping back and forth, a scythe dividing the surface of the churning river, and then he felt something massive slam into the back of his legs and for a moment all he could hear was the river rushing into his ears and mouth.

It was too cold beneath the surface and the man spun in the current for a moment until he could figure out where up and down had gone and it wasn't until he reached out and pushed his body upward from the rocky river bottom that he realized he had let go of his son.

He surfaced to a high, keening scream. The river was moving faster, so fast, and the boy was drifting out to the middle and the man saw that the boy had found use of one arm and so the man yelled out, "Grab hold of something, now! I'm coming!" and the boy wouldn't stop screaming but he heard the man and reached out with his good arm as he drifted and moments later managed to hold fast to a patch of downed conden vines.

"That's good! That's good!"

The man dove forward into the water, some part of his mind wondering where the fish was, and how fast it might be, and why the back of his legs were on fire, but the only real thought in his head was an animal prayer on repeat.

Please, my son, please, my son, please, my son, please…

The man was fast, and the prayer was meant with all his heart, and he was nearly to the boy but the river had grown too deep below him to anchor his feet and when he surfaced he realized the current had pushed him just past his son, still screaming, still clinging to vines, and everything was too late because the boy saw the man and reached out for him and the man reached back but their hands would not touch with the river turned against them and all that was left for the man was to be a witness as the great gray fish which had hunted them broke the surface and opened its jaws so wide that the boy's outstretched arm slid into its throat and the boy was still looking to his father, still reaching, when the creature closed a mouth full of razors over the child's head and shook to tear free what it had claimed and dove to the murky river bottom with the boy in its maw.

No.

No.

No!

And the man dove beneath the surface to undo what could not have happened but in his rage and shock he had not drawn a breath so his chest burned for air. Still he swam deeper but the demon was so fast and strong with the current at its back, and the evening wind turned the riverbed into a rotten churn so that the man could not see beyond his arms and there was a bright red color swirling before him that could perhaps be tracked but that would mean acknowledging that the boy's blood was joining the river in great volumes and so the man surfaced and scanned at a distance for the fins of the bullheaded devil which had taken his son.

In seeing nothing he knew at that moment that this was the death of his family entire, that he and his wife had time remaining but no life to fill it with. But this thought could not save his son so he shook his head clear and breathed as deeply as he could and dove back beneath the surface.

Big fish pin their prey to the bottom and keep feeding. Grandfather told me that. There's a chance.

There's a chance!

The man swam to the bottom of mid-river where his eyes could tell him nothing and swept his hands back and forth in the blackness, finding only smooth stone and the broken branches of long-fallen trees.

He surfaced for air, and dove back down again.

And

Again

And

Again

and

Again

For so long anyone watching would have thought him mad, swimming deep and searching the blackness until he felt he was floating in the void of space and the cold would soon crush his lungs while his limbs flailed.

He was so small. A beetle pinned to a board, inverted, legs running nowhere.

He was nothing.

He looked in every direction.

There was nothing.

Oh, god.

No god. *Nothing.*

Nothing. Nothing. The boy: gone.

His boy.

Dead.

So the man thought to grab the heaviest stone he could find, to set it on his chest and let the weight hold him down until he stopped knowing this was a world which had existed, but the fire in his lungs and the strength left in his body betrayed him and he found himself at the surface of the river, drifting until he came to rest against a piling of rocks.

The man simply breathed—his body demanded it—and there was a blessed moment where he was numb and his eyes took in the dusk light as it settled across the river and lit fire to the leaves of the trees swaying along the western bank and he thought for a moment that his dark prayer had been answered and the world might be undone, taken into the sun and burned clean.

But then he looked to his empty hands and realized it was the same evening light he'd always known, moving now across a world in which nothing of consequence any longer existed.

I've got you.

The man screamed then, his face lifted from the stone, the sound animal and separate from him and granting no escape.

Dusk stretched into night as the man lay across the rocks, the coldness of the surging river the only feeling pulling him from a nightmare vision he could not remove from his world:

The jaws open wide, a wall of consumption crashing over the boy.

Was the boy still screaming as the fish closed its mouth and brought the world to its end?

How long had he screamed? How much had he understood in that moment? How merciful had the first snap of those jaws been? Had the boy continued screaming as the creature dove beneath the surface and swung its head from side to side in victory?

What did the boy see? His father, reaching. The endless throat of the beast. How much more? Perhaps it was so fast that he saw nothing. Knew nothing. *Please*.

If I had brought more water…

If I had watched him closer…

If I'd denied him the bow…

If I was to him faster…

If I was stronger…

If I could have…

If…

I did not love him enough. I failed.

The man did his best to stand, then walked toward mid-river, legs heavy from the cold forever in which he had lain as wreckage against the rocks. With movement feeling returned and he reached down to touch the skin across the back of his legs, stripped and raw from the assault.

It watched us. It hunted us. It could have just attacked me, my legs in its jaws.

It wanted the boy. So small. So easy to take.

It ate him. It ate him. The boy's heart is still in its belly. Are his eyes open inside…

No!

The vision was across the man's eyes again, his boy in the thing's mouth, and he wondered if this was a hell in which he was trapped, to ghost along the river for eternity, set upon by his waking nightmare.

It had to end. He would be free of this. He would call down death and submit to it.

The beast which started this would set him free. It would be hungry again soon. The man's blood was already in the water, seeping from thin tears across the back of his legs.

More blood would be needed.

There was a cleaning knife among their gear on the shore, but the land seemed a distant world to which the man could never return, and so he dove. He searched blind and worried for none of the things which might have scared him from the night river on any other occasion. Death was welcome in any of its forms. The driving cold was a mercy, drawing away his heat and giving him less of the world to feel.

Finally! A stone sharp enough to slice his finger as he drew his hand across its edge. Perhaps the beginning of arrow work abandoned and thrown here as a miracle. The man rose to the surface.

The moon was ascending over the distant rolling hill they called The Sleeping Giant.

The creature would hunt again in the cover of night.

And so the man held the stone as tightly as he could in his right hand and brought the sharpest edge to his left forearm and pulled downward for as long as his body would allow it.

The cold of the river could not calm the fire which flared to life in the man's arm, but it did its best to carry the blood which followed.

The man found a mossy boulder where he could sit with all but his head submerged, and he watched the river roll away from him and waited for the devil to return.

The man wept and prayed quietly for death and did his best not to think about or remember anything else, but the world intruded in the form of a long ululating call that echoed down from the high hills above the river.

Searchers. Sent from the village.

Of course they'd been dispatched. A man gone this late into the evening was nothing. But a man and a child…

Don't call back. No response gives them reason to slow. Could be a trap below. Could be another tribe lying in wait, Urutru poised high in the trees with poisoned arrows, ready to reignite the fires of war.

Even slowed and cautious, the man knew they'd find him eventually, perched as prey on his river rock, and upon finding him they'd pull him away from death and wrap him in blankets like shrouds and bring him home.

Home without his son.

Home to the boy's mother…

She was so full with the child, even early on. There was sickness, but there was also a glow to her, always, as she changed, and when he held her close at night there was an electric field that rolled in waves from her body as life grew inside.

She has so much power now. Look at what she has done.

Even though it tired her quickly, she still hunted with him, and tended crops, and fished, and they spent early evenings talking of the life their child would have, and even then he knew that her love for the new life went far beyond what they'd known together. He heard her quiet singing at night and knew it was meant only for the one in her womb, the one she caressed and carried and gave her life to and smiled at the thought of even when he grew large and his kicks took her breath away.

She'd birthed the child on a full moon, in a hut with the elder mothers who tended to her and rubbed her with oils and spread pulped leaves on her brow and her belly to quiet the pain. Still, the boy was so large that she'd torn and lost more blood than she should have, and she was pale and slow to move for a week after. She'd given so much of herself to him.

It had to have been a month later—another full moon had shone its bone-white light on them that evening—when she told the man how much she loved the child. They lay at the edge of their hut, heads clear of the cover and looking to the sky. The boy was at her breast. She kissed the boy on the back of his head and turned to the man.

"If he ever dies, I'll kill myself."

"What?"

"It's the end if he dies. I won't be able to bear it here. I love him too much."

She stated it as fact. The sun shines. The wind blows. If he dies, so do I.

That was when the man came to understand that some part of them had already disappeared as this new life passed into the world. They'd become a nurturing breast and a protective shell and wisdom and love, but their lives were the child's now and they prayed at his altar.

There were times, later, as they moved past the immediate survival of the child and felt they were man and wife again, when that moonlight discussion seemed an absurdity against the way they were all alive as a family, but in the early morning dark the man still saw the way she had looked beyond him at a possible fate.

I won't be able to bear it here.

I love him too much.

She did love him too much, and that was truth, and now they were all dead, save for the act of dying.

You didn't love him enough. You didn't protect him.

But you can protect her. Let the boy's absence remain forever a mystery. Do not return to tell her what happened. Avoid the gnashing and wailing, the ashen quiet after the boy's name is said. No ceremonies. No fires. No final truth. How long do you want her to live in this new world? Do you want her to feel *this*?

There's the truth, and there's you in a world where the woman you love knows you failed her and that her child died an awful death, and there's her body in the jungle, swollen purple, throat filled with poison leaves, blue lips stretched thin around her final wish.

Or: you disappear. She suffers terribly—that's also the truth—but with time, maybe, maybe, it passes and she lets herself believe you met another woman, or fled to another tribe…something that makes it so she can keep living. She's still young…maybe…

The man couldn't bear to finish the thought, but the truth was still the truth. This was the only way she would survive.

So he decided to disappear.

He moved to the clearing as swiftly as he could, stumbling despite his urgency. The long cold, the shock, the lost blood, all of it a curse now that death was denied.

He gathered enough gear to grant him another day's survival. One pack over his shoulders. A length of rope stripped from the netting. An iron flint. Two of the fish they'd caught and cleaned, and the knife he'd gutted them with.

Had that great beast followed the scent of those slaughtered fish upriver? Had he called the demon with the ritual he'd wished to teach the boy?

The boy.

No. Don't think of him. The emptiness is a shield.

But the boy's bag sat on the ground before him. The man lifted it and the boy's scent came to him, another ghost of the old world, and the man felt it like a wound throughout his body, a tearing from inside his bones.

An ache to hold the child once more.

Another call from the searchers rang out. Branches snapped as they widened their phalanx beyond the trail down to the river. Too close.

The man threw what was left of the day's trip, including the boy's bag, into the river. The current was up—he hoped it would carry their gear all the way to the ocean, where no one could give it any meaning and no word would reach back to his village. He vowed to follow it for as long as he could, and quietly fled into the jungle and the night which cloaked him.

He made good distance using fear as an engine. The searchers would have to move slowly and deliberately, while he was burdened by nothing other than the pack on his back and the wounds across his legs and arm. Movement erased thought and that was a kindness. He ran when the trees above him left enough space for moonlight, and otherwise kept a steady trudge.

After an hour of moving as swiftly as he could a curtain of stars shot across his vision. It made no sense—the forest canopy was so thick here that even vines had abandoned the floor. He stopped and swayed and looked to his arm. Coated in blood, a new slick sliding over the old, mosquitos hovering at the trough. His heart pumping double from his escape.

Start a fire. Seal the wound.

But he knew fire would signal the searchers, and they'd find him, and in his running and the boy's absence they may think him a murderer.

But you are, aren't you? You killed him.

No. Don't let in those thoughts. Fix your arm and keep moving.

Both he and the boy had to disappear or it was for nothing.

It is *for nothing. The boy is gone and you sure as placed him in the mouth of the beast.*

And the man said, "Please, stop" aloud though he didn't know who he was speaking to, and the sound of his own voice, so weak, set him to aching again.

Action—Find horse hair leaves by the river bank. That's good. Can't boil them. Can't set them in the sun to tincture. Use stones to grind them, as many leaves as you can find. Mix them with river water. Grind again. Apply the paste. It burns. It needs to burn. This will cleanse me. This will work. Across the legs, too. Tears there were deeper than expected. They would scar. The devil's mark, always there. Arm still bleeding. God, they'll find me here, pale as a bleached skull, the boars and birds at my corpse. Seal the wound. Open the pack. Nothing sharp. Maybe the side pockets, something from an older trip to the river. Please…There. A finery made of tortoise shell. Her comb.

Her.

You'll never see her again.

Don't think of it. You can't. Break a tooth from the base of the comb. Sharpen it as much as you can against your makeshift mortar stone. A pinprick to the finger draws blood. Strip twine from your rope. Thinnest thread you can find.

Tie it off. Two tugs of the line against the tooth. It's tight. Roll the sharpened tooth in the dark green pulp.

There—a patch of moonlight. Move to it. Sit down. Don't brace yourself. Don't anticipate the puncture. Just push and push and the skin will yield.

Even with the horse hair leaves to cleanse and numb his arm, each puncture brought those nerves back to life. The tooth was too thick and the twine too rough and the man stopped to breathe as stars fell across his sight again. He looked up to the suffocating canopy and pictured the sky extending in long purple waves above him and he thought, "You deserve this pain and any more that comes" and he returned to work, knitting fiery blooms across his arm until he pulled closed the wound and collapsed.

Sun through the leaves—fluttering light across salt-crusted eyelids. A sweet moment of consciousness without thought, born into a world stripped of memory. Then...

The boy.

And the man rolled to his side and emptied his

stomach. He wished that his mind would ride out on the wave of expulsion, purged onto the forest floor so that his memories would empty and be absorbed into the soil, pulled down by rain into roots and spread across the grove of trees until it was transformed into nothing resembling any part of the world he now endured.

He felt crushed, a bug gone belly-up after being swatted to the ground, but another flash of bright morning light across his eyes spurred him to motion.

Day.

Day meant the search party was back in motion, having extinguished the campfire that kept the jaguars and pumas at bay. Day meant he was hunted. How long had he lain there, blessedly numb? They would not be long in finding him now.

The man sat up to stars and waited through the whooshing sound of his heart in his ears for sight to return. He leaned on his arms to get his legs beneath him and felt tearing and fresh warmth. His sutures held but would not yet bear weight or use.

Flies buzzed by his ears, circling for a chance to drink from him, to lay their children in his flesh as it died. Other animals would smell the injury soon. He imagined larger predators were already watching, ready to bear tooth and claw for a chance at his body the moment his weakness was apparent. Everything around him was heat and hunger in motion.

Consumption, he saw, was the only law.

He felt blood running down his arm, dripping from his knuckles. He felt a pull in his heart toward the blood which the river had stolen from him.

What if that feeling was the boy, somehow still alive, lying on the riverbank, waiting for his father to come and dress his wounds and hold him safe once more?

Maybe.

Maybe! He'd heard a story as a child: a villager thought dead in the jaws of a caiman croc returned to his tribe after a week in the jungle, the corpse of the croc trussed and dragging behind him.

Maybe.

Please.

Something could have happened. The boy could be...

But thinking of the child brought the vision, and

the grief, and the man resolved that motion was the only course.

The arm was beginning to scab again but the man could not bear the feeling of air moving in the open wound so he laid freshly torn horse hair leaves across his makeshift stitches, binding them tight with another stretch of twine in crossing X's.

He gathered his pack and considered the two fish inside, and how famished he must be, and how he needed to grow new blood to replace all he'd lost. If he didn't eat the fish soon they'd spoil and sicken him. But he felt no hunger. None.

He placed his hand on his stomach. *Am I a phantom now? I must eat.*

He reached into the bag and felt the cold scales.

He caught these.

A proud smile. A good day.

No.

The man's hand recoiled. He shouldered the bag and did his best to steady himself on empty legs.

A branch cracked in the distance. Perhaps it was

the search team. Perhaps something else, sensing the movement of its prey.

If they find you, she'll know.

With the thought of her he felt a pressure at the base of his neck and his spine, pushing him forward.

He thought, *I must be swift*.

So—despite knowing it had been surrendered to the Urutru long ago, despite the rumors of poisoned traps, despite the fact that it bordered the dark house of the Cuja—the man decided he would cross territories and follow the Messenger's Path to the sea.

The man's father had told him of running the Path as a boy, of how the villages along the river had fallen in love with the pale man's plenty and had worked together to deliver all the rubber they could. The Path was created in a time when the rubber was believed to have no end, so they'd trimmed back the trees and lined the trail floor with buckets of the thickened sap that hardened and made running and travel far faster. Commerce and communication flourished along the Path for years until it finally became clear that a sickness had crept in to the forest and the trees were dying in droves, leprous pieces falling away, open sores black-rimmed where they were tapped too deeply and too often. Then the harvest became smaller and smaller until old tribal wars ignited afresh around the last good trees and the territories were redrawn and declared sacred. Then a few pale men lost their heads to the conflict and the rest of the barons fled with all they could take from the poisoned land.

The tribes remained of course, shedding fresh blood in the dead forest, running nighttime raids along the rubber path. The man's father would tell him nothing more of this time.

The fires of war burned for years, until too many losses turned the tribes toward treaty, and a generation later most remembered only this lesson from the conflict: Fear the others. Stay to your land.

That was the lesson his father had taught him. They'd found the trail once, while hunting. They were tracking an arrow-struck peccary. The boy was entranced by his task, searching for hoof prints and blood, when his father reached out one hand and placed it across the boy's chest.

"We stop here. You've done well, but the peccary

is lost to us. This is the Messenger's Path before you, and it leads to death."

Now the man worked from those memories in pursuit of the old road. The sun was high when he finally saw a thin gap in the trees across the way, the canopy still divided by the ground cleared for the Path.

He traversed the river at a slow section embanked by dry rock, but toward the middle of the crossing the cold suck of the water over his legs made him moan.

This current pulled him from me. We didn't respect it enough. I should have…what?

I should have paid more attention.

The thought a knife in his chest. He shook his head from side to side and stepped onto land.

Far enough downriver, and now I've crossed. This is their land.

He knew little true of the other tribe, nothing that he'd verified with his own eyes, but the childhood tales were enough to speed his heart: They eat

their enemies. They burn you first. Brand you.
Play games with you. Torture you. Surround you,
laughing, and stab you over and over and over
while their women cheer them on.

I should turn back.

But then the man realized the fear was something
from his childhood, a vestige of the old life he'd
shed in the river: He would suffer now. He would
die. It was certain. And what of it? So long as his
wife was spared the truth.

He could still hear the river when he came upon
the Path. He looked down the length of it and
found it smaller than he'd remembered. The
jungle was already swallowing the old road. Vines
and bugs and beetles worked ceaselessly to return
the sick trees along its border to the soil, and the
thin rubber Path had weakened and crumbled as
fresh roots caused rifts and rotted branches fell
across the way. But it was still there.

*It leads to death. But even if the Urutru deliver my
head to the village, my people may believe the boy
escaped.*

There was a feeling that swept through the man
then, cold as the river that had pulled at his feet,
and he realized that he'd never been so alone and
that no one could help him, and he thought

of his wife's embrace and tried to remember it exactly as it had felt two nights ago, before the great bullheaded fish rose from the river and tore him from the light in which he'd lived.

Nothing. He could not find a sense memory of that old world. It would not penetrate the gray shell he felt extending from his skin, keeping the warmth away.

She must never feel this.

Disappear.

He looked to the Path once more and believed that the grace of his own death lay ahead somewhere between this jungle and the sea. The terrible beauty of that thought gave him the strength to run.

The fear and exhaustion were a blessing. There were stretches of time outside of mind where the world was only the man's bellowing breath and the sound of each foot striking the old rubber trail. His sight drifted out to the ground ahead of him and only snapped to attention when sound or movement betrayed the approach of some hungry beast. Sweat mixed with jungle humidity until he felt as if he was running through a cloud of steam. When he was parched he made brief sojourns to the river, cupped his hands, and filled his belly short of sloshing. He gained speed as the sun fell and the dusk light weaved living shadows across the trail. He felt his pulse inside his head and it beat as strong as ever and he knew he was alive but he also felt a madness encroaching because he could see the entire jungle thrumming around him with each surge of blood through his skull.

He wondered if he was even himself anymore or had become something small beyond measure, some element floating without will through the tributaries of a great green heart.

It was, at times, a lonely feeling. At others it was freeing to believe himself only a mote of matter moving without consequence or thought.

He did his best to remain in this state until night fell, and memory returned and crushed him staring dead into the smallest fire he'd allow himself.

He thought the day's run had given him distance on the searchers, and wondered if they'd even pursue him along the trail. When he heard movement before dawn and a high-pitched whistle then he knew he'd been spotted.

Damn this fire.

But he didn't recognize the whistle. Too high. Too long. Not of his tribe.

Urutru?

And though he'd found little sleep and spent the overlong night haunted by visions of the boy and the beast, he knew he had to return to the Path and hope that he wasn't being driven into slaughter.

With each stride forward into the dark he anticipated their attack. He pictured the dart striking his back, the way he'd curl on the ground spitting red foam after he'd bitten through his tongue. He waited for the spikes which would snap and swing down onto the trail and run him straight through. Or worse—a net would drop over him and he'd be captured and tortured and they would laugh at what he'd become.

This is the man who fed his son to the great fish!

He ran faster, until dawn came and he felt he had placed some distance between himself and those who followed. Those who might somehow know what he had done.

He was starved—his belly showed its first signs of life by tumbling over itself and clenching on burning acid. His lips cracked and bled. The leaves he'd tied over the wound on his arm were crusted with blood at their edges, but a thin yellow fluid trickled from underneath the dressing whenever he ceased running. He knew the gash was unclean, but he couldn't stop long enough to let flies deposit their children to clean death from the wound. He recognized few of the plants in this alien territory and if he sought to treat himself he might succumb to poison as soon as heal the damage. He looked up to the sky.

Grant me time. Let me run further from this place.

The sky gave no answers, and the man's head swam from thirst and exhaustion so at first he wasn't sure what he saw swirling above him. He blinked his eyes and focused.

Three white-throated caracaras circling against a yellow dawn. One pinned back its wings and dove.

His grandfather's lesson: *Caracaras follow the kill. Sign of the bird could mean something fallen and fresh to take back to the tribe.*

The man could not bring himself to eat the fish in his pack—he was sure they were rotting by now anyway—but if there were a peccary or bush pig or capy where the caracaras were landing, he could scare them away and strip the meat and smoke it at nightfall and do his best to continue down the trail without dying from hunger.

The man's arm throbbed. A thin string of drool ran from the corner of his mouth. He left the Path in search of anything that would help him find his way further down the river.

Not food. Nothing fresh, at least. The terrible smell hit him before he even saw the birds flapping their wings at each other, trying to decide who would be the master of this kill. A maelstrom of squawking and beaks aimed to draw blood. Feathers and dust drifted into the river, swirling out and away on cold eddies.

Closer. The three birds sensed him and shifted from circle to line, regarding the new threat, not yet ready to leave their meal. The largest of the three let out a screech loud enough to scare smaller birds from their morning rest. For a moment the sky above the river was dark with wings.

The man held his ground, then stepped forward. *Maybe the rot hasn't yet reached the inside of the kill. Maybe there's still a heart or liver warm inside the corpse. I don't need much. Please.*

Two of the birds spread their wings as he approached. One extended its neck and turned its sight on him.

They're as hungry as I am.

He looked to the ground, seeking a suitable stone to throw at the gathering. But if he failed to strike the largest and frighten them away, what then? Could he fight off their beaks and talons in his diminished state?

No. They would tear him to pieces and the jungle would feast upon him in order of strength.

Give them the fish!

But he *caught them. That was one of the last good things he knew of the world...*

The man was frozen, but then he pictured the boy and his mother together. First the baby at her breast, then the boy in lap, lulled through a fever by her songs and the gentle touch of her hands.

He pictured her knowing she'd never hold the boy again.

He held onto that thought and used it to force himself to remove the pack and bring it in front of him and unlatch the thin bone clasps and pull free the fish.

He laid the fish on the rocks before him and opened his arms to the birds. An offering. Then he slowly backed into the tree line and waited for them to smell their favorite prey and move away from the old kill.

After a time they found their courage and abandoned one dead thing for another.

The man collapsed to the rocks. His hunger and any other thought of preservation were shed the moment he knelt before the kill and realized what he had found.

Was this all that remained of the boy?

A portion of his arm, still attached at the shoulder, though the shoulder met nothing but empty space and torn white skin and the jut of broken bones. A pile of swollen offal which swayed as the river's current failed to pull it free from the rocks on which it was ensnared. And there…separate from the rest and torn deep through its palm where the boy had tried to push away and found only the teeth of the beast…a hand.

His hand.

The man reached down and swept up the boy's hand in both of his own and though it was too light and too cold and smelled of death he brought the hand palm-first to the side of his face and held it against his cheek and let loose a terrible animal noise that sent even the ravenous caracaras skyward.

With time—who knows how long—a sense of the world around the man returned to his mind and threatened to pull him from his mad reverie. The man fought.

No.

The boy is here.

His hand is on my face.

But the hand is so cold. It never moves.

No heartbeat. No heat.

I'll warm him. Just give me more time.

But too much time had passed. The man's scream had rippled through the green hell around him for every living creature to hear and all the while he'd sat there on the rocks with his eyes closed against the world.

He did not know the Urutru were upon him until he felt the razor-tip of a stone spear press against the hollow of his throat.

Madness became a shield. The man thought first to drive his throat onto the spear, to be done with the world at last. But the madness sang to the man, and told him the boy was still alive in the belly of the beast.

The hand at your face is cold but the other is still warm, still attached to the boy's beating heart. And you will save him. You will strike down the great fish and you will pull your child free. You will be together again.

So the man opened his eyes on the Urutru, but he looked through them to the Path beyond. There were five bodies which stood between him and the Path. They would not stop him.

He looked at the leader of the men, at the tremble in his spear, and said, "You're not really here."

The leader yelled something the man was surprised he could understand and drove the tip of his spear just far enough forward to tear the soft skin at the base of the man's throat and send a trickle of warm blood running down his chest.

The man smiled at the leader—what threats could they offer more terrible than the world he already knew? He gently grabbed what little wrist was still attached to the boy's hand and moved it down from his cheek. He had pressed it there so firmly and for so long that a print remained. He could not stand the feeling of the hand disappearing from his face, but the men before him needed to understand.

The man held the boy's hand out in front of him and looked to each member of the tribe.

He pointed with his free hand at the ground between them.

"This is your land." They returned prideful nods.

"But this…" The man looked to the small hand held out before him. "This is mine. It is my world, my hell to bear. You don't exist here. We are ghosts passing. Your land, your cares…they mean nothing to me. You mean nothing."

The leader of the Urutru swung back his spear and brought it sweeping toward the man in a wide arc. The man did not move, or drop his eyes, or let go of the small hand borne before him. The wooden staff of the spear struck the man's head and sent him staggering to the side. Just as quickly he recovered and was walking back toward the tribesmen with the hand outstretched, blinking away fresh blood as it ran across his face.

Even the leader stepped back.

"Strike me again and I will pull you through to my world."

The man pushed the boy's hand closer to the leader's face.

"I will find the fish and I will save my son."

And with that the man walked passed the Urutru and left them staring at the river, each feeling forever cursed as the ghost disappeared into the jungle behind them.

The fever which protected the man's mind and the fever which branched out from the man's chest and pulsed at the seeping wound in his arm were not the same. While one drove him further down the Messenger's Path—to find the fish, to find the child—the other sought to slow him and burn out the river of rot running a canyon through his flesh.

The man drank all the water he could. He cupped his hands in the cool river and poured them over his aching skull and tried to ignore the tremors he saw running through each arm.

He felt himself covered in a slick of sweat and river mud and seep and feared that he might drop his son's hand and not know it had slipped away. He delicately wrapped the hand in dried pulcha leaves and stripped another thin tendril from his rope to tether the package to the inside of his bag. He set the hand down lightly in the base of the bag and sealed the top.

There you are now. You are safe with me.

The hand pushed him forward, guiding him to the rest of his son.

There was only the trail and sound of ragged breath and the sense that the Path would carry him to the moment he needed, when his arms would again fold around his son and hold him close. Then the sun crested and the man felt the jungle close around him, a moving, airless grave, a tapestry of interwoven vines and teeth that narrowed before him like the back of a cave.

Head swimming, vision covered by an impossible snow, the man felt his skull tighten until he thought it might cleave and spill his mind across the cracked rubber of the Path. Sweat stung his eyes and the wide cracks in his lips. Barely able to detect the shape of his damaged forearm, he still noted that death's dark colors swam out from beneath his leafy bandages.

The arm is killing me. There is no more time.

The man staggered to the river on too-tired legs and collapsed at its bank. He used his good arm to push his other dying limb into the current of the river.

Please. Clean the wound. Cool me. Save me. Please.

Give me something back for what you took.

But if I can't be saved...

Am I far enough from home? Will the birds and boars come quickly enough?

Let me disappear here, if I can go no further. Or bear me up, and let me find the great fish, and the boy.

The boy.

The man reached back and tried to free his pack so he could open it and empty it into the river so nothing of the boy would be found, but the sun overhead pressed down harder and hotter and the man ceased to move.

His vision narrowed further until he could see only a thin stretch of mid-river, the sun blindingly bright off its surface. The man felt his heart beat and stop, then rush ahead to catch up. He had believed that one day he might meet death in peace, he and his family prepared for him to leave, whatever he'd built for his family passed on. But this death was what he would receive. Collapsing under the sun, pulled to the ground by a poison arm, the boy still waiting for him downriver, trapped in the beast.

A silver-headed beetle with black armor crawled

on to the man's shoulder and turned toward the wounded arm in the river.

It begins.

He followed the beetle with his eyes, down to the water's edge. There the leaves wrapped around his wound pulled loose in the current and swirled out and over the smooth stones of the bank and then drifted toward the middle of the river. The man's eyes stayed there and his thoughts scattered as if each was carried away on those lost leaves, waves of Please and No and Why and I can't move and Let me die and Let me rise and always The boy the boy the boy spinning out and away from him.

The sound of the rushing river became a torment. Time was broken. The man was broken. But the river acknowledged neither and carried on as it always had and would and the sound of it was the song of nothing caring and the man knew it would be the last thing he'd hear.

When the white bird sailed down and landed on the river the man thought this might be some final grace. Perhaps the bird had come to deliver him from his shell, to pick free his soul like a seed and carry him away in his beak, flying to the next world.

But then the man saw those terrible gray fins rise

in the river behind the bird. So large, so far apart.

The fins disappeared beneath the water without a sound. The man could imagine the blunt bull's head of the thing plunging forward with new momentum, its mouth opening and flooding its stomach with fresh river water.

How cold that must feel to the boy.

The man tried to yell, knowing he could not bear witness again, knowing that this was a world long ago given to devils which waited for each of us, but there was little left of the man to cry out and the river was calm for a moment and the bird sat still and never saw the wave of black death until it erupted from the river beneath it and took it in its jaws.

An explosion of feathers and water and blood rose with the fish. A single wing pushed against the wind while the rest of the bird tumbled into the throat of the beast. The fish twisted in the air above the river, its belly hideously full, threatening to burst, the sun bright against its slick whiteness for a flash before the weight of the thing and all its prey slammed back down into the rushing river and disappeared into its cold, muddy depths.

This will happen again and again. I'll lie here petrified

and watch the devil feed and it will never end.

The man imagined the boy inside the creature, reaching out to him, pushing against the wall of its flesh, trapped in that darkness forever.

From behind the man came the sound of laughter, dry and crackling, a beetle-blown tree collapsing in the forest, and beyond the man the river ran ever-on and sang him the song of nothing caring, so when long, bony fingers wrapped around his face and held a smoke-scented cloth over his mouth and nose he knew that the devils would never be done with him.

The blackness was a mercy until the memory fell over him like a spell.

They'd been hunting fruit that day, only a year ago, picking around the old groves, the man seeking to tire the boy with all the walking so that the whole family might sleep through a single blessed night.

The boy pointed to a small fruit hanging on the

tree ahead of them. "Is that a nispero?"

"No, it's a lulo. Look at the orange color. How round it is. Nispero will be brown this time of year. Gather it still. But be careful…"

"I know, I know. If the hairs break off on my hands, I must not rub my mouth or eyes."

The man made a face like he disapproved of being interrupted though in truth he was proud: the boy had been listening, and learning.

The boy pulled down until the lulo broke free. "Got it!"

"You got it. Now place it in the basket and let's keep looking for nispero. I promised your mother."

"She loves nispero! She eats it so fast it gets all over her cheeks."

"Yes she does. So let's not come back empty handed. She'll kill me."

A look of concern from the boy. The man smiled. The concern disappeared.

They pushed back into the grove, beyond where anyone had cleared away the leaves and broken branches and fallen fruits swarming with ants. The air cooled there and the smell of sweet rot brought hovering clouds of tiny flies which stuck to the sweat on the man's brow. He crushed them and wiped them away.

The boy was ahead of him and crouching before something on the ground.

The smell of rot had changed from sweet to foul.

"What is this, dad?"

A small oncilla cat lay matted to the forest floor. A wound to its shoulder—perhaps the bite of a puma—looked to have finally claimed it. The black eye facing them had shriveled gray and maggots were at its wounds. The stomach of the thing bulged, and the man was thankful the boy hadn't investigated the body with a stick—one poke and the cat's side would have ruptured and covered them both in the scent of its death.

"Oncilla. Hard to tell when you see it like this."

"Can we help him?"

"No. He's passed on."

"Dead?"

"Yes. Dead."

"What will happen to him?"

The man tried to picture any benefit they might gain from the find, but he was certain the meat had soured and at this point even the small fur wasn't worth skinning. "Nothing. He is gone. His body will feed the soil and bugs, and once that bulge in his side opens the birds will come and clean whatever is left."

"But he was here, before this?"

"Of course. He existed."

"Existed?" The boy raised his eyebrows.

"He lived. He was alive, like you and I are alive right now."

A shadow slid over the boy's face. His eyes looked to the side, no longer meeting his father's. The man thought it best to keep the boy from staying in that state.

"Now what's in your basket?"

The boy looked over and in. "Two lulos. That good rock I found."

"No nispero?"

"No."

"NO NISPERO? AYE! YOUR MOM NEEDS THE NISPERO! LET'S GO!"

And the boy seemed to understand: that their lives continued and they left the dead behind and kept searching for whatever was next. But the shadow didn't leave his face until they returned to the tribe and the boy ran to his mother and leapt into her lap and began to cry.

"What is it? What's wrong?" She ran a soothing hand over the back of his head and rocked ever-so-slightly.

The boy sniffled and wiped away his tears and looked up at his mother.

"I wish I never existed, but now I do and now I have to be dead."

And the mother did all she could not to show the pain in her heart across her face and she rocked him faster and said the only thing she could think of as a wall against his truth.

"Not for a long time. You, and me, and your dad, we all have a very long time to live. I promise. It's okay." She closed her eyes and pressed the boy's head against her chest so that her heart might calm him. "It's okay. I promise."

Bound in the darkness/No body to hold him.

He was alive/This was the afterworld, a distant circle of light surrounded by ashen black stone.

The roof of a cave, a small hole at the top of its dome/The eye of an old god, its gaze on him unwavering.

An old woman, clicking as she moved, enrobed in leather strips which bound a shell of sticks and jagged bones to her body/The moving tree, shaking whatever the man had become, swirling smoke over him until he faded into nothing.

Time seemed to pass but the light above him never waned. It was not the sun. Any heat he felt came from a nearby fire but nothing flickered against the walls of the cave.

The old woman licked her lips, a hollowed shell in her hands dripping silvery water/The moving tree hovered over the man, branches for arms, and lowered a shell to his body and tilted it so that the water foamed and three black leeches spilled over its lip and onto his chest.

A hole opened in the middle of the tree and it issued a command: *Drink from him.*

The man felt the leeches squirm against his skin—*my skin*—and he searched for the will to move but he was still too weak and something held his arms to his sides.

Vines? I'm not…I'm not dead.

The man turned his head toward the swaying shape which stood over him. Branches rose above the shape's head and clicked against each other as it moved and then it bent toward him and the slightest light showed him an ancient human face.

Not a tree. A woman.

The woman moaned low and her eyelids fluttered open and shut and her upper lip curled back to reveal a row of sharp black teeth.

Not a woman. The Cuja!

In his terror, the man found the will to move. He strained against the vines, felt bamboo pressing against his back.

Trapped. She'll have my heart for a meal.

The Cuja laughed.

"I have no use for your heart, but I will take payment."

She pressed a cloth over his mouth and nose and the man held his air until his vision disappeared but it was no use and soon he was breathing in the smell of smoke and old soil and blood, and then the moving tree was above him again and it held a skinner's knife in its branches and it bent to work under the eye of the old god.

The man figured himself dead again when it saw the tree lift his ravaged arm and swollen half-black hand to its splintery mouth. It seemed to sniff at his fingers and pause.

"Two of these are rotten, and even the bloodworms won't save them. The smallest finger has some life in it yet. This will be my first payment. Our covenant will be found in this."

The moving tree pressed the blasted hand against a perfectly round stone and with one swipe of the skinner's knife it severed three fingers from the man's hand.

The smoke had done its work—there was a fire in the man's hand but it was as distant as the idea of the mouth he might have used to scream. The man's eyes were just as lost to him so he was unable to look away when the clicking wooden beast brought his smallest finger to its mouth and began to chew.

The sound of crunching bone echoed against the blackened stone walls/The Cuja had taken her payment.

In the cave beneath the jungle floor, in a world outside of time, the covenant had been set.

In memory again, he held the boy's hand. The boy had begun to walk and he and the man moved in circles on a well-trod path. A warm wind blew over them. The man smiled down at the boy but the boy only looked ahead, intent, everything in the next step. At a rise in the path the boy lost his footing and grabbed the man's hand tightly to prevent a fall.

The man woke in darkness to the feeling of that hand grasping his, pulling down. Needing him to hold on.

A pain spread through his chest and he knew it would never leave him. He feared it might tear him in two. He hoped it might tear him in two.

The Cuja stood over him and ladled water into his mouth. It smelled musty and foul but his thirst overcame his disgust.

"Good. *Good.*"

She laid a cool cloth on his forehead, the sticks bound to her forearms scraping against his scalp and threatening one of his eyes.

She leaned in closer, her sour breath on his face. Her eyes were heavily cloaked by wrinkled lids, but there was a gentleness to them that confused the man. "I have lifted the smoke from you. You may speak." She smiled then, but the sight of her jagged teeth reminded him of what she'd done, the sound of his flesh as sustenance.

The moving tree. She's no woman!

"I am neither. I am both. You will see me here as your mind allows."

What? The devil's tricks...

"No devils. I am the Cuja. And I would prefer you speak. Your thoughts come to me as screams. My head swims from them."

The man tried to clear his thoughts but in his panic a memory found him: his grandfather's voice. "Those woods are hers, and hers alone. If any child should wander her way, we find their body at dawn, heart missing, eyes gone white. The Cuja gives bad magic and takes your soul as payment. She works for the Urutru. She helps them hold their dominion."

The Cuja laughed, a dry cough. "Such foolishness is thought to be the provenance of children, so why does it always spill from the mouths of old men? The jungle takes children. Men take children. And I offer loyalty to nothing so small as a tribe."

She punctuated the last of her sentence by poking at the man's belly with the sticks jutting from her arm. Something attached to his gut slithered back and forth at the disturbance.

The leeches. What is she doing to me?

The man recoiled as much as he could, but when he shifted it felt as if the vines binding him wrapped tighter.

"Be still! You've barely returned to this body. I'm not certain you're alive just yet."

Stop, please. This is *bad magic. She's trying to confuse me.*

"You were already confused. I found you by the river, mind lost, chasing that sad beast."

The Cuja's eyes had again taken on a softness. What *kindness* could she feel for that terrible creature?

The man could no longer stand the offense of her intrusion into his mind. He did his best to speak.

"Not a 'sad beast.' A monster."

She clicked her tongue and shook her head. "No *monsters*. A *shark*. Only a shark. A living thing like you. But her mind, like any held by this world for too long, has broken. All that remains of her is hunger. That is its own madness."

A rage welled in the man's chest. To speak of his child's murderer in this way! He turned toward the Cuja, straining against the vines to spit in her face, to tear loose and grab the old devil and...

The Cuja waved a hand through the air, the

shadow of it a tree falling across the wall of the cave. With this motion the creeping plants which held him pulsed twice and knit against each other and forced the breath from his chest. The leeches on his skin wriggled as his trapped blood surged to the surface of his skin. He was bound too tight and his head swam with the sound of the rushing river.

The Cuja smiled. "Look at you. Look at you!" She leaned over him, her sharpened teeth hovering above his face. "You are as mad as the shark. Ready to destroy without thinking."

The man could not pull a breath into his chest.

Please. No air.

Please.

The Cuja waved her hand the other direction. The vines loosened, but not much.

"There's a poison in your mind which clouds everything. It brought you here. You believe a child, *your child*, is special. Yet you have the smell of the hunt on you. You would kill a child in your hunger, as would most."

The man found he could breathe again and felt he must say something against the black spell the

Cuja was weaving. "A child? From hunger? *Never*."

"What perversion of the world do you see in which humans bear the only children? In which only man could carry grief or wail into the night?"

The man had no answer. He knew the jungle fed upon itself. He knew his people were of the jungle, and ate as they were eaten. All the people of his tribe knew it—it was why they woke on moonless nights to the slightest sound beyond their huts.

And yet when he thought of the boy, of his wide eyes and the sweetness in his voice and the way his tiny feet kicked against the man as the child slept between his parents, he could not see the jungle.

The boy was more. The boy was a new heart, beating fast, spinning beautifully. The boy was a fresh mind and gentle hands. The man loved the boy, and that was no poison. The time before the child seemed a shadow. Time with the child, even in all its need and worry and sleepless nights, seemed the bright of day.

Tears came to the man's eyes. He was grateful that the anger had returned to sadness—it was what he would have of the boy until the moment they were together again.

The Cuja reached down with her hand, sticks scraping the man's scalp. She pressed one dry, cold finger to the corner of the man's eye until it welled over. She returned the wet finger to her mouth and wrapped her lips around it like a suckling pig and closed her eyes.

She shuddered, then looked straight at him. A dim purple light curled in the blackness of her pupils.

"You are sicker than I'd imagined. So much life ahead of you and you believe yourself dead. The boy's heart only ever beat in time with his mother's, and even that passage was fleeting. After that his life was the world's to unfold, same as yours. But the pain has stolen all reason from you, left you ravening for the impossible inside of it. You will not be able to hear what I am saying, not truly. But there is purpose in you still. I felt a storm aching in my bones as you and the shark entered my territories. Your paths were not meant to diverge, not yet. And so I will mend you and grant you passage through my land. I will give you what you seek."

Is this a cruel trick? A game? The man thought of his rotten hand, of his fingers fed into a splintering mouth, teeth crunching on bone. *Is this a seduction to indebt me to the Cuja until she desires to eat the rest of me?*

"You forget that I hear you even when you do not speak. And if I wished to eat any more of you then you'd already be picked clean, skin drying over smoke. Waste no more of my time. We enter a new covenant. I know what you wish, but it must be said in breath. So tell me what you seek."

"I seek only the boy."

"And what would you give to find your child?"

"Anything." The man thought of the boy's body in his arms, how tightly he would hold on to save him from falling, how their hearts would press together. "Everything."

"Very well then. That should suffice."

The Cuja turned from the man and he heard dry shuffling sounds and smelled cave dust and heard the sound of a wooden cage unlatching and creaking open.

Something snorted behind the man, took four reverberating footsteps, then moaned and stretched. The man heard its joints cracking, the sound of rocks unmoored from the cliff side and crashing down. The thing behind him snorted again, an awful, wet sound, and this time the noise came from far above the man's restrained body.

"You are needed now, Mactatu." The Cuja spoke, a sweet lilt over a stern undertone which told the man she had no room for error in addressing whatever it was which stood behind him. "The bloodworms alone cannot save him. There is death in his arm, and it must be removed."

The man heard the patter of saliva ropes falling to the cave floor. He smelled rot upon rot.

"Eat only the death. The rest of the arm is mine."

I've been betrayed. It was all a game. The cruelty of devils, to dangle hope before me and strip it away. And now they will feast.

Then a rag was over the man's mouth and nose and the smoke was thick in his mind. He saw the glint of a sharpened blade and then for only a moment that metal showed him the reflection of the thing which stood behind him. His vision could not separate tooth from fur from pulsing grey mass and surely his mind would have fractured then, had it not already been lost along the river.

The Cuja's hand tightened on the rag. Her teeth scraped against each other from the effort, knives on knives in the ever-shining light of the old god staring down from above and the smoke entered the man's blood and there were mouths sucking upon his blasted arm and he heard a strange wind blow through the moving tree and it said *Hush, child, hush now, or this feeding may never end.*

He was alive and free in the darkness. Nothing held him and the feeling of his breath against one of his arms told him this was not the release of death. He pushed up with his hands and felt the dirt of the cave floor shift beneath his fingers. Without light his body could not figure out exactly which way was up but he let the pull of gravity in his bones guide him.

There was no pain in his spoiled arm. *How could that be?* He ran his other hand over the surface of his arm and found it oddly numb but still present. *Not eaten.* And there were two spots where something hard and small jutted beneath the surface of his skin.

Bad magic to help me mend?

"Hello?" His voice echoed on stone. Maybe they were just saving him for another meal. But they had him laid out for the slaughtering. They could have slain him then. *They.* The man thought of the thing she'd called the Mactatu, then did his best to push it from his mind.

"Hello?"

This time a voice responded. It reverberated from each wall of the cave, surrounding the man.

"You survived, then. I had worried. It was difficult to separate the Mactatu once his tongues had wrapped around your bones. His eyes told me he thought it would be a mercy to finish you off, but I know he's hungry more than anything else and saw through the ruse."

The man felt phantom tendrils of the thing's intrusion into his body, memories which even the smoke could not conceal. "Please speak no more of that creature."

"Fear of being penetrated. Fear of being fed upon. Ha! How fragile is the world of men? Mactatu saved your life, and I have nursed you here for longer than you're capable of understanding. You should be grateful that our covenant is so well met."

The man remembered what he had been promised. The boy! To be set back upon the Path!

Could this be real? If it was, he must return to the river as fast as he could. The beast, the thing the Cuja called shark, would be so far down river by now…

"No. She has barely moved since I found you. You feel as if you are under. Your mind understands the idea of a cave. But you are...*outside*. Time does not flow through these places."

The man grew frustrated. Each of the Cuja's words felt like a spell or a puzzle. "If I have done my part for our agreement then I must be on my way. If the boy is close then I will find him. I need my bag."

"You do not need the bag, or anything from it. I have prepared you for your voyage."

*But the boy's hand! It was wrapped in leaves, tethered to the bottom. It was all I had of him and...*he's dead he's dead he's dead, I should have buried the hand, I should have buried all that I found by the river before the birds returned to eat him, before the Urutru saw what was left and spread word, I should never have taken the boy to the river at all because that beast lay in wait and the boy was in its mouth—NO!...*and I must bring his hand to him. When I find him.*

A weight pressed down on the man. *Have hope again. Or find a dead place and feel nothing.*

The Cuja spoke from all directions. "I have restored your body but it is clear your mind is still lost. You cannot stay here any longer."

The man shook loose his thoughts of the boy. *Focus. Now. She's setting me free.*

"I cannot see," he said. "How do I find my way back to the river?"

"Sight does not matter where you are now. There is no light in between these places, but if you walk and your mind knows you are walking, those steps will take you back to your world. You will reach a clearing and beyond that you will find the passage to the space above."

"How will I know when I am in the clearing?"

"Light will return to you. And you will find two altars. The first holds the Horn of Procne. You must place your lips to it and force your breath through to show that you have accepted our covenant and returned to time."

"And at the second altar?"

"A gift, of sorts. You will see."

"And what do I do with this gift?" His voice had no echo this time, and the Cuja gave no response. There was a low rumble the man felt in his bones, and he could not tell if it was the growl of something in the dark or perhaps the walls of the cave falling and the blackness opening up around him. Since allowing either truth into his mind would leave him paralyzed there in the emptiness, he chose instead to put one foot in front of the other and hope that the ground itself did not slip away.

The clearing revealed itself step by step. No matter which direction the man turned to walk, his feet always landed in the center of the clearing. He stopped walking from frustration, feeling this may be a trick of the Cuja's, and that she was laughing at him from some distant corner of her world, but then he realized he only knew he was in the center of a clearing because a low, red light was glowing around him.

He took another step. Again his foot landed in the center of the clearing, as if the ground was moving beneath him, but the light shone brighter.

Another step. More light.

Another step. The walls around the clearing came into contrast. The red light shone off a surface which shifted around him, a perfect dome of hard stone overrun with moving vines. Water seemed to run through the cracks in the stone, defying gravity, feeding the foliage. Flowers spun open slick and dripped clear fluid from their pistils. Pods released spores and insects gnawed at leaves or each other, and the man wasn't sure if he should take another step. The brighter the red light became, the more the life surrounding him twitched and grew and hungered.

How long until they see I'm here?

He looked away from the seething walls and to the sandy floor beneath his feet. He took one more step forward and as his foot landed dead center the sand rippled and shifted around him in concentric circles, a wave of particles rolling away from his body.

She sent me here. To be swallowed. Is it quicksand?

Something emerged from the sand in a small circle around the man, a glint of white bone pushing up beneath him in every direction, and the man pictured the teeth of the great worm which was about to pull him into its gullet and he thought *I'll know how the boy felt. This is the Cuja's second altar. This is her gift.*

The man closed his eyes against the abomination and only opened them when he realized he was still standing and the sands at his feet had calmed.

Not teeth surrounding him. Skulls. A ring of tiny birds' skulls, each with their eye sockets pointing toward him at center.

One of the skulls had a small sigil on its forehead.

Is this the 'Horn of Procne'?

Maybe this was simply the first gate of the clearing, and he needed to pass through it to find the altars. The man took another step. It landed where it had left. The light grew no brighter.

He squatted in the circle of skulls and reached out toward the one which bore the mark. Nothing reached out to strike him. He rested his hand on the skull. It felt cool and smooth. He looked up at the mass of writhing, growing life over and around him and hoped that these skulls were not some kind of protective seal which he'd be breaking. Then he lifted the boney mass from the sand.

It was heavier in his hands than he'd expected. It carried a low vibration, a hum which shot through his hands and caused him to shiver. And then he noticed how suddenly the clearing had gone silent. The life around him was frozen in place. The man heard not a single sound aside from his breath.

You must place your lips to it and force your breath through to show that you have accepted our covenant and returned to time.

The man did as he was told. He found a small hole at the base of the decorated skull, pulled in all the air he could, placed his warm lips against the cold death of the thing, closed his eyes, and blew.

A light, sweet sound filled the air, the call of the first bird of morning. The sound made the man think of new sun on his skin, of moments spent lying beside his wife and child and knowing they'd soon wake. His heart thumped in his chest, a new ache on top of the old ones, and he opened his eyes to see the Horn of Procne turn to sand in his hands and run to the ground.

The other skulls around him did the same, disappearing into the floor of the clearing.

The man looked to the walls of the clearing and saw that the life there had resumed its tumult.

He stepped forward and this time his foot landed ahead of the other. He had passed the first altar.

And what had the Cuja said of the second altar?

A gift, of sorts.

The man looked for anything else other than sandy floor and writhing walls. The red light had no source and cast strange shadows in every direction.

One of the shadows stayed in place and as the man got closer it remained—a hole in the cave wall large enough for a puma to pass through.

Some kind of trap? Or the home to something larger than the things which cover these walls?

The man circled the entire clearing and found nothing else. As he walked the sound of the moving things all around him reached a fever-pitch. A buzz joined in and the tone caused the man's chest to tighten and a cold sweat coated him and he realized this was not a place for any human to stay.

What if this passageway closes while I'm here? What if that small cave or tunnel or whatever it may be is already shrinking?

And time is passing now. I can feel it in my chest. Which means the creature is headed downriver again.

And so the thought of the boy and the shrinking world around him forced the man into the hole, crawling toward the unknown.

When the man was able to stop slithering on his belly and finally found himself back on his hands and knees it was a huge relief. When the tunnel finally opened on another dome, this one smaller and walled in by dark, wet rocks, the man was able to speed his pace. He saw torches burning in the middle of the cave, forming a circle of light around a dark shape on the floor. He knew torches burnt down with time, and the man could not bear the idea of being thrust back into the dark next to whatever *gift* the Cuja had left for him.

As the man got closer to the second altar, he was not sure he could bear the idea of receiving this gift at all. The torchlight revealed a shape he knew well—an open grave. He was only three when he saw his first grave filled and would never forget that feeling of holding the rope, helping to lower his cousin into what seemed an earthen mouth, and how they had all helped his aunt shovel fresh soil into the grave until the white shroud over the boy was covered and gone.

But the man also knew that the Cuja would not release him from this place unless he accepted her gift, so he returned to his hands and knees and crept slowly to the edge of the grave.

It can't be the boy. Not the boy. Please, not the boy.

The man peered in and then felt relief followed by a wave of guilt. The shrouded figure was the size of a man.

Not the boy, but who am I to feel joy at the passing of whoever this may be?

Above the man's shoulder, one of the torches flickered, then died.

Time.

"What else must I do? I accept this gift."

Another torch spluttered, then flickered out.

He could feel it in his blood, what she wanted from him. He felt controlled by her even now, beyond her straps and smoke and whispers over sharpened teeth.

"I can't."

Another torch died. Soon the cave would be black and the man would be trapped there, starving, alone with the corpse, while the boy drifted further and further away.

So the man lowered himself into the grave, reached out with shaking hands, and peeled back the shroud to see his own face staring dead-eyed at nothing.

And the man knew it was sorcery of some kind, but the face was perfectly his and he was confused because he thought he should feel some great sadness to see himself dead, or perhaps revulsion or relief or anything other than the fury which rushed through him.

"You. *You.* You led him to the river. You could have watched him closer. You should have known, but you failed him and you fed him to that goddamned devil. And now he's gone and you won't even let him die! You could have buried what you found, but you left it to the birds. You're chasing ghosts. You have forsaken your wife, and she must be in panic or grief or both by now. The Cuja asked you what you'd be willing to trade for the boy and you said 'anything' and meant it even though others love you and have been true to you. What have you done? You are hiding in shame. Running away from the truth you owe your wife. You're not saving her! You're saving yourself from the pain of her death. You fucking coward. You lack the courage to kill yourself. You did this!"

And the man was lost to his anger and balled his

fists and brought them down into the dead-eyed face beneath him and there was a rhythm to the pounding that echoed the man's thoughts which were only YOU. KILLED. HIM. again and again until the torches which had extinguished above the man roared back to life.

In the new light the man was able to see the damage he had done. His knuckles were cracked and swollen and the two hard shapes he'd discovered on his repaired arm had trickles of blood spilling away from them where he'd split the skin over whatever the Cuja had sewn in to mend him. And the corpse beneath him was stranger still. Where the man had expected to see a bloodied face he found only a hole where the face used to be. The man's hair lay limp above the emptiness and the man's chin stuck out below it, seemingly still flesh, but the center was only a crater of sand, spilling down toward the middle.

He leaned closer to be certain he was seeing things properly. That was when the hands of the corpse tore free from their shroud and grabbed the man by the arms.

The man struggled against the grip but the dead thing felt like it was made of iron, a machine pulling him closer to the body.

The sands in the cratered face swirled, and

bright blue water bubbled to fill the emptiness. The man lifted his head but he knew he had no choice in this world, that the work of the Cuja held sway on this dominion. His corpse held him tighter and closer until he started to sink into its body and he could feel the waters which had at first filled the face of the thing lapping against all of him. And then his own face was submerged in the whirlpool and water filled the man's ears and nose and he held his breath for as long as he could before he ruptured and the Cuja's gift came rushing into his mouth.

He tasted the river on his tongue, as sharp and cold and filthy as it had been on the day he took the boy fishing. With that taste he felt himself drifting blind in the current. Though he could see nothing, he could feel himself moving and spinning until the motion of the river ceased at last.

It was then that the voices began their testimony:

We told him to stay off the logs. Of course we did. Doesn't take much for the waves to flip one right on top of you.

We respected the ocean and punished any foolishness in its presence. Even took the switch to the boy for pulling his little sister out too deep one morning. Poor thing couldn't even swim yet. Only by the grace of God that she coughed up that water. Our pastor's child drowned in his own bed at night, even after his parents saved him from the tides. You can drown slowly on land, if you take on too much. So we made our girl sleep face down that night. Stayed in the room with her. Must have patted her back a thousand times, to be sure.

We thought the business with the boy and his sister would be the end of his foolishness on the ocean. Surely he feared another round with the switch. Then, one week later I saw him standing on a huge log, and I yelled for him to come in, but he wouldn't. I turned to his father to go grab the boy and when I looked back the log had rolled and I could see the waves crashing over.

By the time we reached the log there was no

sight of the boy. Nothing at all, but waves upon waves and that log, rocking back and forth in the sea.

They say I passed out into the ocean. Landed in the sea and they pulled me up and carried me in and I coughed up my own water. I remember feeling so angry at the men for pulling me back.

I had wanted the sea to wash me out to my son, wherever he had gone.

If we hadn't taken the switch to the boy, would he have come when I first called?

Why didn't he come back to me?

She was born sick. Water on the brain. But she grew. We had birthdays. One. Two. She was sweet. Funny in her own way, though she would get so mad too. It was hard sometimes. Most of the time, really. But we figured it out.

She got sicker, close to her third birthday. I told the doctor there was something in her chest making it hard to breathe. "Probably just a cold," he said. I told him we had to head two cities north that weekend, on account of her father's job. Doctor told us it was safe to travel. "Hold her upright, she'll be fine."

I tell myself I should have felt her breath getting shallow and slowing down. I had my arms around her. But the road was rough and the horses were loud and the wagon shook terribly. I thought she was fine. Leaning her body against me. Resting. But when her head dropped forward, the way it was hanging so loose, the way it dropped so fast, I knew. I knew right then.

They stopped the wagon and did what they could for her. I watched them and didn't say a word, even though I knew she was gone. "Let them try," I thought. "It'll make them feel better."

We buried her in her favorite dress. It was the only one that didn't make her scream when she was alive. She was a particular child.

My husband blamed himself. His job. Never heard another word from him after the funeral. He disappeared. I could not be bothered to look for him.

We were both in our cups and it was the same old routine where he wanted to have a go and I only wanted to lay still and do my best not to lose my dinner. Besides that, I knew my daughter would be awake soon enough. She seemed to wake up twice as early, crying and hungry, when I'd had too much to drink. And what would people think, with him sleeping over at the home of a freshly-widowed woman?

Only it wasn't the same routine, not really, because I didn't truly know the man. Didn't know how cruel he was, or how drunk, or what he was capable of doing. I should have sensed it when he slapped me, but I only wanted him to leave.

I must have thought he left. I swear that's the only way I would have been willing to pass out.

When I think back I realize it wasn't the door to the house slamming. It was the door to the baby's room.

The jury never believed me, but I didn't hear a thing after that. They said she would have screamed, from the pain of it. But maybe he held a pillow over her head before he was on top of her. I hope he did.

Is that the worst thing I've ever hoped for? It has to be. But it's true. I hope that he suffocated my little girl before he split her in half.

Maybe there can be mercies like that in the world.

He wanted to leave for the war. I told him he was too young. He told me they needed bodies over there and turned a blind eye to your age if you were ready and willing. I told him I'd seen the boys that were coming home. If they weren't dead, they seemed to have changed for the worse.

I knew he'd always wanted a horse, more than anything. He'd drawn them as a child and helped to care for them as a boy. Rode in his early teens and helped at the stable with shoeing and bucking hay. So I spent more money than I really had to get him the mare.

I couldn't have known she'd be so testy, so quick to react. It was only later I discovered she'd been used in the war by courier troops until she kicked a soldier's jaw sideways. They decided she spooked too easily and sold her off to the broker who brought her to me.

Had I known…

The boy one property over was helping his father, shooting at the red tail hawks that kept killing their chickens. Our mare had never learned to steady at the sound of gunfire. She reared back, then fell on my boy.

After the fall my son lost control of his legs and arms. His speech came in brief spurts, if at all. His eyes looked through me.

He needed so much from me that I turned back into an earlier version of myself. He was my baby now. I put his toys on his lap while we sat at tea. I fed him with his baby's spoon wrapped around my finger.

I had no idea how much all of this was hurting him until the day he managed to slur out "No." and push aside the spoon with his face.

I wasn't enough for him, and no one would buy the horse so I could have money for an in-house nurse. Then came the nights when he got worse, and the spinal infection spread, and I secretly thought it was a blessing. His disease. Him finally dying.

Once he was gone the guilt crushed me. I'd bought him the horse. I'd wished my boy dead.

I collapsed at his grave. After lying there a while I pushed piles of soil in with my hands. I turned to the others behind me for help, but they demurred. They didn't understand.

When I arrived home that night I walked out to the stable and shot the horse myself.

Thing is, we had that swing going back three generations. Replaced the rope twice, the wooden seat once, but it was sound. And we had plenty of tumbles but nothing like this before, so it wasn't something we worried about. Part we didn't think about was how all those kids, all those feet dragging across the ground, how they kind of hardened everything underneath. Put less dirt between the soil and the big, old rock that was waiting under.

The boy was up early with me. He helped with the cattle and did a fine job so I told him to take a break. I heard him hollering from the swing, but it was a sound I knew. He was having a good time, and I was busy. You're never short for work on the farm. But then I heard the cracking sound and I knew something was wrong. You can just feel it. So I looked over and the branch was still there and there was a drift of dust, but I couldn't see him through the weeds.

I gave him about two seconds to pop up, brush it off, give me a wave. When that didn't happen I rushed over. Saw his hand first, limp in the dirt, then his head. All the blood. Once I saw his head I knew we were too far from town. I

cursed myself and went to him and saw his eyes
and the light was already out.

That rock was always there. Decades. Then one
day my son takes a little tumble and it's waiting
for him.

When I can stand to think about it, I like to
think he got distracted by something beautiful
and that's why he lost his grip.

Maybe a bird.

The sun through the leaves.

Something.

I took my son to the river, to teach him how to fish.

This is my voice.

The day went well. My son was strong, and smart. He listened and helped me sweep the banks for crocodiles. We used paraja leaves to slow the fish, and caught more than I'd expected. We sat in the sun and fed ourselves.

This is my story. It is a poison in my mind. Why must I hear it?

It was a hot day and I failed to bring enough water for the trip. I was distracted by my pride and I didn't watch the boy closely enough.

What gift *was this parade of death? What good does it do anyone to know the unending cruelty of the world?*

I didn't know the boy drank from the river until it was too late. He was mid-river, learning how to use a bow and arrow, when he realized the paraja leaves had made him sick.

Please. I've lived this in my head a thousand times.

The boy had known. He had sensed something when we first approached the river. But I didn't listen.

This river is death.

I tried to get the boy out of the current. I had him on my shoulders, headed toward the bank, when the bullheaded devil knocked us into the water.

The boy was sick from the leaves. He could barely swim. I found him downriver.

I swam as fast as I could. I reached out to save the boy.

And then sight returned to the man and he saw

a woman clutching a baby's spoon and weeping
a puff of dust drifting away from an empty
swing
a log rolling in the waves
a crib with a bloody blanket hanging from its
railing
a woman searching for the one small dress her
daughter loved
and then he saw the boy, his hand outstretched,
r e a c h i n g
for the man,
finding nothing but razor-sharp teeth as the
terrible beast claimed its prey.

And it was too much.
And the awfulness of existing in a world where
children could be eaten in front of their fathers
pressed up from the center of the man and came
rushing out of his mouth in a

gush

of

bile

and

river

water

and washed away the smashed sand-shaped face
of the
shrouded corpse which once resembled him.

And so the man had been returned to the altar
and the Cuja's gift had been received.

From somewhere behind the man there came
the sound of rocks tumbling. Sunlight flooded
the cave, so the man crawled from his grave and
followed the brightness back to his world.

Back to the Path, and his son.

He could run again, even though he had swollen fists and three missing fingers and there were two hard nodules on his arm which seemed to be pressing their way out of his skin. These latter seeped thin trickles of blood, but it felt like a scratch compared to the devastated arm he'd carried along the Path before the Cuja found him.

His fever was gone, but his mind still raced along the edges of delirium.

She is sending me to my son. She has promised him to me. And if she could save my arm—as surely dead as anything has ever been—then perhaps there is still hope for the boy.

The man ran on, feet callused thick as leather pounding the rubber path. His stomach did not speak of hunger, though he couldn't remember the last time he'd ate. When he stopped for water he felt whatever the Cuja had placed inside his arm pulling toward the sea with its own urgency.

She is guiding me. Our covenant stands.

More blood fell from the man's arm. The skin tore with each moment he strayed from the Path.

Bruises flowered dark beneath the surface to let him know something was rending inside. He thought it dangerous to stop moving.

The covenant stands—but what more may she ask of you?

The man ignored the question and sped his pace. Sweat popped and dried across his skin. The corpses of tiny insects and salt-sweat patterns laced his skin. He thought he could smell ocean air in the distance.

He felt the pull in his arm and for the first time in two long days it was toward the river beside him rather than the sea ahead.

I have caught up to the beast. At last.

So he ran toward the riverbank, slowing as he approached the water, thinking he might need to surprise the great fish as it fed.

And then what? Do you understand the size and strength of this thing? The Cuja said it has gone mad with hunger. How can you stop something like that? You have nothing, not even the knife from your pack.

He realized he'd also lost his wife's tortoise shell comb. He had nothing left of her. *Had the search team returned empty-handed yet? What must she feel in the absence of the world she'd known?*

The man's arm thrummed and pulled him from his worry, nearly dragging him to his left along the riverbank. When the violent sensation passed the man stopped and scanned his surroundings.

No activity on the water. No fins or broad, flat snouts seeking the surface of the rolling river.

He'd been brought here for something...

There's purpose in you still.

Then he looked a little further down the muddy red riverbank and saw what he was brought here to find.

There, tumbled among the rocks, bobbing up and down with the current, was their family's bow. The arrow was nowhere to be found, separated and likely shattered long ago.

What is this? Another cruelty from the Cuja? Another gift?

The man walked closer.

I have no arrows. I have no need for this.

And yet the vibrations in his arm had calmed for the first time. He was meant to be here.

The man knelt and picked up the bow. As he gripped it he saw the boy's face beaming, his pride at having caught fish for dinner, at being allowed to hold the bow and arrow.

This was the last thing to bring him joy. This was the last thing he loved.

The man knew what to do.

The answer was in his body—he felt it before he thought it. And so he turned away from the river with the bow in his hand, and walked into the jungle. He found a quiet clearing, the kind his boy used to play in on a peaceful afternoon, where even the evening sun could shine through and warm his skin, and the man dug his bare hands into the soil and cleared out a small pit and set the bow inside the hole. Then he knelt close to the soil so that he could smell it and feel its moisture, and he curled his arms around the loose dirt and pulled it gently and slowly back into the hole. Once the dirt was packed down tight the man rested his arms and face against the grave and sobbed and wept and moaned until his body told him it was done.

After a time he stood and returned to the Path, knowing that some small corner of his madness was lifting.

Knowing that his boy was dead.

And knowing that he must find the rest of the boy.

His arm trembled at the pull of the Cuja's magic. There was purpose in him still.

Another day on the path. His heart was heavy, but his body held strong. He never felt the urge to eat and wondered if the Cuja had planted something in his belly to fill him through, or stolen his hunger with a spell. He had swallowed the river water which surged from her "gift," but in the end it had filled him with voices rather than sustenance. He could make no sense of it. But what sense was left in *this* world? Having seen the world below, the realm which held powers like the Cuja and creatures like the Mactatu, the land the man thought he knew sometimes felt like a sorrowful dream.

It was a relief to feel so small. To bring his pain

down to the scale of his existence. If he was nothing much, then what of his suffering?

Sometime in the night, perhaps drawn out by the moon, the rigid bumps under his skin finally ruptured and pushed through. He had not noticed, nor stopped his gait, and so whatever was revealed was quickly covered over by clotted blood. He had to admit there was now a relief, like an infection finally lanced, though the low hum of the arm still pulled him forward.

He watched the dawn creep in and smelled salt air and he saw signs of other humans along the trail. Bags abandoned, or left for others. Lost shoes and broken bottles. The sun crawled upwards and was at its zenith when the man realized he was almost to the city where the mouth of the river fed into the ocean.

He tried to walk, to be cautious, for he had no idea which tribe controlled this territory, or what they might do if they discovered him.

He tried to walk, but his arm had its own gravity and pulled at him with such strength that he was forced again to run.

He heard the chains first, before he saw the fishermen. The sound was a terror, louder than the river, louder than the ocean beyond it.

Hundreds of heavy chains slapping to the ground, slashing through the water.

His arm had brought him to the edge of the jungle, where he could see. The entire village was at the river mouth, or the beach, where a festival was taking place. The man could barely hear the laughter of children—unaware of the world, free within it—and distant music. He smelled fish being smoked inside banana leaves and finally felt hunger stir in his gut.

Men lined the banks of the river, some of them waist deep where the muddy waters roiled against the counter-currents, some of them holding onto the top of reef fishing nets, the rest holding and thumping chains against the river and the rock breakers and the reef itself.

The man barely recognized their style of dress, though some had adopted the clothing of the white men who had come for their rubber trees. He listened to their voices but could not identify their language over the cacophony of the chains they were using to drive fish into their nets.

He looked down at his muddied tan shorts, his

overly-thin frame. He felt his matted hair and ran his hand along the protruding, crusted bumps on his arm.

He would not be welcome here. Why had the Cuja send him down *this* path? To show him how the world moved on without him or the boy as part of it? To watch these men care for the work of fishing while their wives and children played in the sun? Always more cruelty…

The man's lament was cut short by another sound: a scream, high-pitched and horrible, from the muddy river bank.

A group of the fishermen fled in panic, dropping their hold on net and chains.

A fire erupted in the man's arm, and it was his turn to scream. He looked down to see two sharp stone clasps drilling upward, further out of his skin, breaking loose the clotting and sending fresh blood to the sand, pulling something underneath toward the surface.

"I will give you what you seek."

The boy. The shark. They're here.

But what is happening to my arm? Why are there clasps woven into my skin?

Another scream from the river. The man realized that the Cuja's magic had carried him this far. He'd have to trust it a little further, even as it caused him this new agony. The time had come.

The man ran toward the riverbank. The people might not even notice him now that the devil was in their waters.

Between the mud stirred by the current and the fresh flowers of blood in the water, the man could not see much of the beast. But she was in the shallows of the river now, near the shore, and he could see her fins cutting back and forth, circling around. *Mad with hunger.*

A fisherman had lost the bottom half of his left leg to her appetite and they had dragged him as far onto the sand as they could before trying to tie off the spurting stump. He was white as bone and far gone, but they would not give up hope.

"Let them try. It'll make them feel better."

These are not my thoughts. The river is still inside of me.

The man was surprised to see that many of the fishermen were still in the water, slowly reeling fistfuls of net towards themselves, attempting to close a circle around the creature. It was possible they had not figured the size of her yet, how she ran twice as long as any of them tooth-to-tail. They did not understand what easy work she'd make of reef netting, how wide her jaws could open when she was ready to kill. But the man knew, and still he walked toward the circle of men, and the fish at their center.

The fishermen startled and closed up ranks as he walked toward them, even as they kept their eyes on the circling beast in the water. They issued a warning and he understood enough of their language to figure out how to gain passage to the water.

He looked at the men in front of him, looked them each in the eyes, lifted his aching, bloodied arm up and placed his hand over his heart, pointed at the water with his good hand, and spoke.

"Que mato a mi hijo. Voy a matarlo."

It killed my son. I will kill it.

A space opened between the men. They nodded.

They understood him. The Path carried the man into the bloody mouth of the river.

He walked straight toward the great fish, his eyes watching her as the mixture of salt water and freshwater and blood slid over his calves and knees and waist.

He knew how fast she could be, how final any wrong move would be. But she did not seem to regard him at all. Rather she keened from side to side as she circled and white membranes slid halfway up her all-black eyes.

He was within four strides of the creature when he finally realized what was happening. More than madness had fueled the shark's endless hunger— it moved now with the hypnotic rhythm and ritual of any creature bearing new life. The water around them both filled with billowing white clouds of fresh fluid. The man felt warmth on his skin and was overwhelmed by the sharp, pungent smell of the shark's birth-water floating to the surface.

As the miasma flowed over his arm he felt something beneath his skin pushing up to be freed. He held his arm out before him and felt its throb. He backed slowly away from the still-circling shark, not knowing how fast she'd recover from the birth, and did the only thing he could think to do. He reached out with his other hand, grabbed the stone clasps woven into his arm, and turned each one a full circle.

A seam split across the skin on the soft side of his arm, two short lines at his wrist and crook, and a longer one nearly the length of his forearm.

Beyond the shock of the strange magic, the man saw the tears in his arm for what they had made of his flesh: *a flap*.

The man continued to back away from the beast, and whatever progeny she'd expelled into the water.

There's a purpose in you still.

And the man knew it must be done so he reached into and under the flap of skin and was greeted by new pain, a screeching in his mind, begging him to stop. He pulled up and away at the loose skin until it hung over the other side of his arm and he was opened and spilling fresh blood.

It was only after he saw what his arm held, beneath the wetness of the wound, that he realized how final his covenant had been. He had offered the Cuja anything and everything, and she would take it if he wished to finally find the boy.

The blade in his arm shone like nothing he had ever seen, even through the blood. The handle of the knife was an abomination. The Cuja had found the boy's hand in the man's bag. She had stripped it clean and smoothed all those tiny bones and bound them together around the base of the blade.

"You do not need the bag, or anything from it. I have prepared you for your voyage."

She made this monstrosity and buried it deep inside the center of his arm. The pull of her magic on the blade had brought him here: inside the murky waters of the mother shark, the boy's hand buried inside his father's body. And the man knew that the only way he could remove the blade and strike down the great fish was to pull it straight out of his arm, through the veins and anything else she'd woven over it for the voyage to the sea.

What world is this?

Then the man looked up and realized that he had lost sight of the beast. There was nothing visible other than the waves and the spreading milky cloud and even the fishermen surrounding them had gone quiet and were slowly backing out of the water.

Then a yell from the riverbank.

"Ahi!"

There!

The man could see fins, but the space between them barely ran the length of his leg.

The child of the beast, already voracious, already searching.

Her child, fed by his own. Her child, foolish enough to leave the safety of the birth-water. New enough to forget the presence of the massive hunger which gave it life.

The man knew where the devil had gone. It had followed the scent of easy prey.

A flash across the surface of the water. The flat wide head of the mother bull snapping from side to side, erupting from the river with the child in its mouth, leaving only a severed tail to float on the surface a moment before sinking back under the water.

At this sight the fishermen lost their resolve to trap the beast. Their circle fell to chaos, each running toward their own safety, their own families, to try to forget the world in which they lived.

The man kept his eyes on the beast and watched as the fins turned toward the open ocean and dropped beneath the surf.

NO!

The man knew there would be pain. But what was pain?

He knew there would be blood, great founts of it. But even blood was temporary.

Nothing was truly his. But he would close the covenant and make the Cuja's word truth.

So he reached into his arm and wrapped his hand as tight as he could around the sharpened cruelty fashioned from the bones of his son, and he pulled back toward his heart through ripping and snapping sounds and then he bled and bled into the water and sent his message to the sad beast which was swimming through the current with the flesh of its own child hanging from its teeth.

Our paths were not meant to diverge.

Come to me devil.

Give me my son.

The man was not certain if the water was cooling around him or if he was bleeding to death that quickly. He wondered if the Cuja could see him now. Did her barked laughter echo against the caves below, knowing that she'd sent him to witness one final attack and then kill himself so near the shore? He couldn't picture it—the sadness in her eyes had never felt a ruse, and she had sent him to his son's bow, and the only burial he might know.

The man waited, vision blurring in salt spray.

The water was so cold. Growing colder. The fishermen watched him, but none came closer or offered aid.

The man scanned the horizon, hoping to see fins heading toward him, to know that the shark had smelled his blood as it washed out with the tide.

Nothing.

The boy is gone.

Then the man heard voices along the pier which split the beach, fishermen yelling, but the man's head swam and it was a blessing that the meaning of words had fallen away and soon the rest of it would be gone too and at least there would be nothing left.

At least this world allows for death, he thought, just as something huge slammed into his torso—*so fast*—and closed its jaws around his opened arm and over his chest, and then the pressure came, a pressure he could barely comprehend. And even though his arm was destroyed he could still sense that his fingers were pressing against the inside of the creature and the feeling was so repulsive that he tried to pull away.

He was underwater next, then pushing at soft sand with his legs and barely resurfacing, and the shark would not let him loose. It would not release the bite yet, not until it could clamp back down and shake and tear. It was weakened by giving birth, but it still wanted to take all of what it had claimed.

Then the man felt something rough brush against what was left of his hand in the shark's throat and even though the beast was trying to eat him he found a thought, clear as day.

The shark's child is still moving. Whatever is left of it is slowly dying next to what's left of the boy.

It's hell in there.

And with that the man knew that this was his last chance to pull the boy free of the dark. *His* child would not be left in this cauldron of death, swimming in decay and falling to pieces to feed this broken creature.

A shock of energy shot through the man's body and flooded his mind with blood and he realized that the free hand holding the Cuja's knife was his, and that the hand which *truly* held the knife was the boy's, and as such it deserved to be driven into the beast with great violence. So the man slashed at its gills, and its eyes, and the shark finally released its bite but it was too late because the man pulled back the knife a final time and swung it down into the creature's wide, thrashing head.

Then, finding the thing properly hooked by the blade buried behind its jaws, the man pushed with his legs as fast as he could to pull the devil to shore.

They'd barely made it out of the surf when the man collapsed. The weight of the thing and all it had consumed was too great. Its tail flopped in the surf, but it was blinded and torn and its gills could pull nothing from the air. The Cuja's sad beast could die slowly. The man was beyond worrying about such things.

The sun was still high in the sky, but light was dimming in the man's vision and he knew what that meant. He slid through the bloody surf around the beast's tail, then crawled up to its head and grabbed the handle of his knife with both hands. He could see the inside of his left arm where it had been flayed open and knew that it still worked only because the Cuja willed it.

He braced his feet against the body of the beast and pulled with his arms and freed the blade from the shark's head.

He crawled back through the surf and slid alongside the white belly of the great fish. He saw shadows in his periphery, but they were only shadows. If they watched him so be it.

The skin of the shark was thick and tough, and the man used what strength remained to saw a slit upwards from the thing's tail. Then he reached into the beast and felt for the hard angles of bone against flesh, and when he found that he slid in the Cuja's knife for one final cut, this one as delicate as he could make it.

The boy's hand was still warm, and so small, and the man remembered his wife then, and how their love had made this hand and helped it to grow, and how they did their best to give their son a world better than the one they knew, and then he thought of the bow he'd buried deep in the jungle and he knew he had to do one more thing before he could join the boy.

The man was cold, but the sun was still the sun, and he felt it on his skin. He thought the boy should like to feel it to, or would have, and so he reached and pulled until the child was loose and in his arms. He pushed aside a sopping slick of the boy's black hair and kissed him on the forehead. The boy was the boy, and he was with the man, finally, and it was time.

The man wove together the fingers of their two remaining hands and closed his eyes and slid into a memory of a better world than the one they'd found. He remembered a morning when they'd lain like this, his wife's hair entangled in the boy's other hand, the boy's breath warm on the man's face. The man woke first, and slowly opened his eyes and watched the boy sleep. Finally, the boy woke, saw the man watching over him, and smiled.

The villagers had kept their distance. First out of fear, then out of respect.

When they finally approached they found the shark vanquished and the man cradling the remains of a child. The blood-darkened sand around the man told them he had died there, holding the boy.

Written in the sand above their bodies were two words: a woman's name, and the name of a village far upriver.

The villagers moved the bodies to prepare them for burial. Then they returned to the beach and took care to write down the names in the sand before the tide came and washed the shore clean.

About the Author

Jeremy Robert Johnson is the author of the critically acclaimed collection *Entropy in Bloom* as well as the breakthrough cult novel *Skullcrack City*. His fiction has appeared internationally in numerous anthologies and magazines. Johnson lives in Portland, Oregon.